FOR THE WANDERERS

Written | Illustrated
Violet Shaw

For you,
Maeve Karlie.

On your first Easter.

If we are an idea,
you are a masterpiece.

<u>A note to the wild wanderers</u>, the young and wise reading this book, and the younger listening:

'For The Wanderers', is written as free verse poetry, with an evolving structure, mirroring a rhythm.
The message from this book, is to find your own rhythm, wherever it may take you.
With that in mind, play, imagine and re-create the rhythm of these stories, in any way your heart leads you.
After all, we all dance to a different beat.

<u>For you, with love:</u>

BOOK ONE | As You Wake

Stories of little animals,
finding their own magic, and learning to be kind.
Just like us.

one. Maybe, Words Matter
two. Oh, Shark
three. Freedom

BOOK TWO | As You Dream

From our hearts to yours.
Words of wonder and hope
as you rest your head,
and become lost in your dreams,
at the end of a long day of adventures.

one. The Stories Surrounding Us
two. All In Your Own Time
three. As You Dream

BOOK ONE | As You Wake

Stories of little animals,
finding their own magic, and learning to be kind.
Just like us.

one. <u>Maybe, Words Matter</u>

There once was a Brolga
and an Emu,
and both were the most beautiful
of beings.

The Brolga had a dance,
that sent hearts into a flutter,
and the Emu
had long, fast legs they all treasured.

Each morning they would meet by the river,
for how else
would they take in their reflections?

And spent hours debating their beauty,
for one of them just had to have more.

The Brolga and the Emu didn't realise,
as they spoke, they were terribly unkind.
Not out of hate,
but indifference,
which is far worse
in the grand scheme of things.
Which turned them
a most awful green.

They soon became the only two laughing.
For their jokes no longer funny,
just mean.
Their friends found them hurtful,
but,
even as they glowed green,
they still felt too beautiful
to care.

One day, along came a Koala,
and the Koala was rather beautiful too.

It wasn't how the Koala looked that drew the appeal,
but instead how they'd glow gold when they spoke.

'I don't understand', said the Brolga.
'How are you so beautiful to watch?
You don't have my wings'-

-'Or my legs', chimed the Emu.
'But you seem the most beautiful of all?'

The Koala paused for a moment
and thought.

Never had they compared
a winged dance to long legs,
nor either to a furry coat.

After a moment,
the Koala continued,
with the only answer that came to mind:

'Maybe beauty cannot be based solely on our shell,
perhaps,
it cannot exist without kindness.

We are only as beautiful as our most hurtful words,
and
we live in a world where words matter'.

HAPPY Bday! ♥ SHARK
GIGGLE
GIGGLE
GIGGLE
GIGGLE
SHHHH-HAHA!!!

<u>two. Oh, Shark</u>

The world can be a lonely place.
This Great White Shark might not have a pack,
but he and his best friend, Seal,
always know where it's at!

Shark and Seal
would spend hours and days
exploring the never-ending supply
of shipwrecks and caves.

On the day of Seals birthday, Shark was excited.
Her perfect present under his fin,
and his best jokes practiced,
down pat in his head.

'This time,' he thought, 'I'll fit in.'

As Shark arrived,
he took a big brave breath,
and began to swim over,
armed with a smile and a 'Hi'.

He was caught of guard,
struck with surprise,
as the other seals swam away giggling.
They had decided they'd hide.

As much as he tried,
he couldn't stop his bottom lip shaking,
and their laughing got louder,
tears tumbled, his heart breaking.

Seal arrived to her party just a little bit late,
and with the sound of Shark distraught, she exploded.
Her laughing party guests had just sealed their fate.
With anger, she roared, they were her friends no more.

Her heart broke, as she cried with her Shark.
There had been no one at the party he could turn to,
and nothing,
now it was over,
she could do.

As his best friend cried with him,
Shark couldn't stop feeling alone.
He could still hear them laughing,
even though Seal had sent them home.

'I-I think it is time',
he stumbled out between sobs.
'To find somewhere I can truly b-belong.'

Seal didn't want him to go, but
understood how he felt.
She wouldn't always be there,
to throw bullies out.
Through her tears,
and her sniffles, she managed to stutter:

'Y-you do belong, Shark!
In the deep ocean, on adventures, with me.
They may not understand you,
those silly creatures,
b-but, I promise that I do.'
You belong with me,
where we can chase the currents
in the great open sea!'

FOR THE WANDERERS

Despite how he'd miss Seal,
Shark decided to venture.
Remembering to pack his best hat
as a good first impression was essential.

He arrived in the shallows, and hit the sandbar,
with a hopeful heart and a *thunk.*

Behind him was his fear,
as well as his sandy back fins,
which he noticed, were now
thoroughly clogged.

He dusted off his suitcase, put on his best smile,
as despite his tails dismay, he'd come such a long way.
He'd get used to the sand, even if it took him a while,
so, he struck up a conversation with a local named Ray.

'How do you do?'
Spoke Shark politely to Ray.

To which Ray quickly replied:
'I do quite a lot,
but you're wrecking my spot!'

Shark sighed and quickly apologised:
'Oh! That's not what I meant,
but, I see what you mean.
I'm sorry for messing up
your lovely garden dream.'

All those feelings Shark had felt at the party,
suddenly began to surface, interrupted only
when Ray rose and concluded:

'All my life I have dreamt of the sandbar,
of how I could glide across its floor.
I don't understand
why anyone would swim out,
it's too far to roam into the great unknown.'

'But, dear Ray,
don't you ever dream of more?
Of great open space, ocean valleys,
shipwrecks and deep sea caves?
Of a world beyond the wave breaks?
There's much more to explore beyond the shore.'

'The world beyond my seaweed
is no business of mine,
and frankly, much too far to glide.
But, if you're here too,
there must be nothing left there for you.
I'd love for you to stay,
I'll make a place for you to settle,
then together we can watch the beach
change with the tide!'

With the kind words of Ray,
Shark felt a warmth in his heart.

As he smiled at his new friend,
and wiggled his sandy tail,
his new joy began to dissolve.
He had suddenly felt a new discomfort,
something he had never felt before.

Without the space of the ocean to swim,
it was a little hard for his gills to breathe.
The sandy floor wasn't the only problem,
but the air above the water.
His tail just didn't fit between
the sandbar and the surface.

His new friend, Ray, had began drawing up a way
for Shark to unpack his suitcase and hopefully stay.
When straight out of nowhere, three turtles appeared,
embarking on their journey, out towards the deep.
Giggling as they tumbled, they climbed his fins and rode each wave!

SQUAAA-NORK!
HELLO! WOULD YOU LIKE TO JOIN SEAL AND I FOR A TREASURE HUNT ON SUNDAY?

As they rolled into the distance, it became clear,
what both Seal and Ray had known all along.
What makes some happy,
sometimes is what makes others sad.
Your spirit can't shine
living their adventure.

Ray had a beautiful story,
of a life in love with the shallows.
A lovely place to stay, but,
Shark, just couldn't thrive there.
He could still be friends with Ray,
for friendship doesn't need two to be exactly the same.

Shark learnt a lot from his two best friends.
Even though he longed for the deep blue ocean,
he could still find joy in visiting Ray
and his beautiful, warm home
in the shallows.

One day, he hoped,
Ray might agree to an adventure.
But, for now,
he and Seal can spend the day,
then swim back out with the turtles beyond the bay.

They all remained the best of friends,
sharing the greatest stories of their travels.
Knowing that their friendship was much more
than just convenience.
It was something real and true.

Just like Shark, Seal and Ray,
we belong around those who make our hearts sing.

It really is OK,
you really don't need to choose one place to stay.
If you are made for the depths,
and they, for the shallows.

<u>three. Freedom</u>

No matter where you are,
whether you go by plane or even by car.
Whether you run until your legs are sore,
or crawl like a lizard along the floor.

If you tumble down a grassy hill,
stumble upon an adventure afar.
Have you ever wondered how high birds fly, or
whether trees touch the sky?
Maybe even peek behind a waterfall,
just in case it hides a secret door.

Your world is as big, or even as small,
as your heart can imagine it to be.
However far you choose to roam,
wherever your dreams may take you,
may you never feel alone,
in the emptiest open plain or
most crowded room.

Remember that love has no boundary
of distance or of time.
Love should lift you, even if
you fear you've climbed too high.
Adventures alone are the best way to grow;
like the wildflowers, you're born to be free.

The same stars will shine
wherever you venture,
holding all of our wishes like secrets.
Roam free, little dreamer
and let the world be whatever you make it.

BOOK TWO | As You Dream

From our hearts to yours.
Words of wonder and hope
as you rest your head,
and become lost in your dreams,
at the end of a long day of adventures.

Let me tell you of those stones,
sitting quietly by your feet.

They have formed over years,
upon years, of change
and of chaos.

If you sit and hold them for a moment,
try close your eyes, if you can.
You can feel the energy from each lifetime,
connecting with your soul.

For everything, even you,
holds something greater
than what can simply just be seen.

We can always learn from every creature,
every plant and every stone.
You just need to listen, so your spirit
can hear the song.

We can learn calm from the sound of a sun shower,
just as we can learn power from a storm.

We can learn control from the difference
in the rain falling through between.

Be excited when someone is different.
They have so many things to share.
Just imagine how boring it would be
if all our ideas were precisely the same.

There are so many things we can learn
if we listen, and if we are present.
This is how we find our voice.

This is how we learn how to speak.

<u>two. All In Your Own Time</u>

Breathe, little one.

You are as perfect as you can be,
for where your journey is right now.

You are not here to chase time,
you are here to create.
To transform the time given to you,
into an adventure of your own.

You are here to be a light
on the darkest days of winter.
To warm the hearts of those
who have forgotten who they are.

To be change, to be hope.
To be wonderfully you.

The reason those around you
forget all about time.

<u>three. As You Dream</u>

Little Dreamer, welcome home.
For you this world has just begun,
and for us, you are now the world.
You have been born with all the time you need,
to make an impact of your design.

May you become lost in the words of great poets,
and know the wonder of adventure.
May you know how it sounds to hear your heart sing,
and be able to share it with those not able to hear a sound.

May you remain beautiful, calm and whole,
in a world designed to break you.
May you grow stronger with each passing year,
and made not for moments of in-between.

May you heal the hearts of others,
with a momentary glance,
and be proof of something greater,
without being reliant on your fears.

May you always find happiness, however far you roam.
And be led by your own spirit, so you never feel alone.

May you be brave.

Brave enough to speak,
to fight for what you know is right.
To speak for yourself,
and to help others find their voice.

To know that you are strong,
and powerful,
and a leader.
Understanding that all of those things
require you to show kindness and gratitude,
because true strength
cannot exist without either.

May you be heard,
and above all, seen for who you are.
To really see someone
is to see into them, to understand them, to appreciate them.
To set aside the noise,
and see their appearance as a refection of their soul.
Not the other way around.
To see someone is to understand empathy.
Empathy is less common than it should be.

You are filled with incredible potential
and we can't wait to see you soar.
May you always know your value; remember,
every success is built by a fall.

Most importantly,
may you always feel loved.
It is one thing to be told,
and quite another to unquestionably feel.
You will always, be loved.

Always.

www.ingramcontent.com/pod-product-compliance
Lightning Source LLC
Chambersburg PA
CBHW071506150726
48000CB00006B/2720